LARRY AT NUMBER 10

E.C. RADCLIFFE

ILLUSTRATED BY DAVE HILL

LARRY AT NUMBER 10

E.C. RADCLIFFE

Matador
9 Priory Business Park,
Wistow Road, Kibworth Beauchamp,
Leicestershire. LE8 0RX
Tel: 0116 279 2299
Email: books@troubador.co.uk
Web: www.troubador.co.uk/matador
Twitter: @matadorbooks

ISBN 97 81800461 789

British Library Cataloguing in Publication Data.
A catalogue record for this book is available from the British Library.

Printed and bound by CPI Group (UK) Ltd, Croydon, CR0 4YY
Typeset in 12pt Bembo by Troubador Publishing Ltd, Leicester, UK

Matador is an imprint of Troubador Publishing Ltd

This book belongs to

Stoke Newington Library

Enjoy the Larry
Magic

I am Larry. I live at 10 Downing Street. My Boss is the most *im-purr-tant* person in the United Kingdom – he is the Prime Minister. This means…

I am the most *im-purr-tant* cat in the country. At 10 Downing Street I am chief mouse-catcher, head of *paw-trolling* and champion window-ledge sitter. Obviously, this is for lookout *purr-pusses*.

The Boss thinks I am

paw-some.

There are other cats on my street.

There's *silly* Palmerston next-door...

Foreign Office

and *lazy* Gladstone across the road.

Treasury

They are no match for me.

Their mousing attempts are
paw-thetic.

Nothing impresses me.

I meet VIPs every day:

The Queen

The President

The Emperor

The Queen is desperate for me to be chief mouser at Buckingham Palace, but I am needed at Number **10**. I am top cat at **10** Downing Street. That was until…

The Boss got a dog called Dilyn.
He thinks we will be brothers.

Purr-lease, have you ever heard of anything so *rat-iculous* –
a cat and a dog being brothers! I think not.
I have an *im-purr-tant* job to do whereas dopey Dilyn…

Chases his tail, guzzles sausage-strings and chews things.

What *paw-sible* job can dozy Dilyn do – Chief Sausage Catcher?

Purr-lease!

But the Boss says, *"You are adorable."*
He takes Dilyn for walkies, gives him
din-dins and tickles his tum-tum.

While I am mousing,
Dilyn is chewing his
squeaky toy.

SQUEAK!

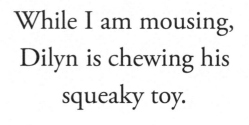

When I am guarding
the big black door,

Dilyn is shredding toilet-paper.

While I am
paw-trolling,
Dilyn is pooping
on the plant-pots.

Dilyn's days at 10 Downing Street are numbered.
Today I have plonked the Boss's shoes and a heap of very
im-purr-tant papers into Dilyn's basket…

He has chewed them into a million pieces. My plan has worked *purr-fectly* – Dilyn is sure to be in the doghouse…

But the Boss says,
*"My poor baby, you must want
din-dins,"* and gives Dilyn a
sausage-string.

Claw-ful! This is not *meow-sic* to my ears.

The Boss is sleeping.

I am standing guard while Dilyn is gobbling a sausage-string.

When *CATASTROPHE!* ... a cat-burglar breaks in

and bundles me into his bag.

And guess what...

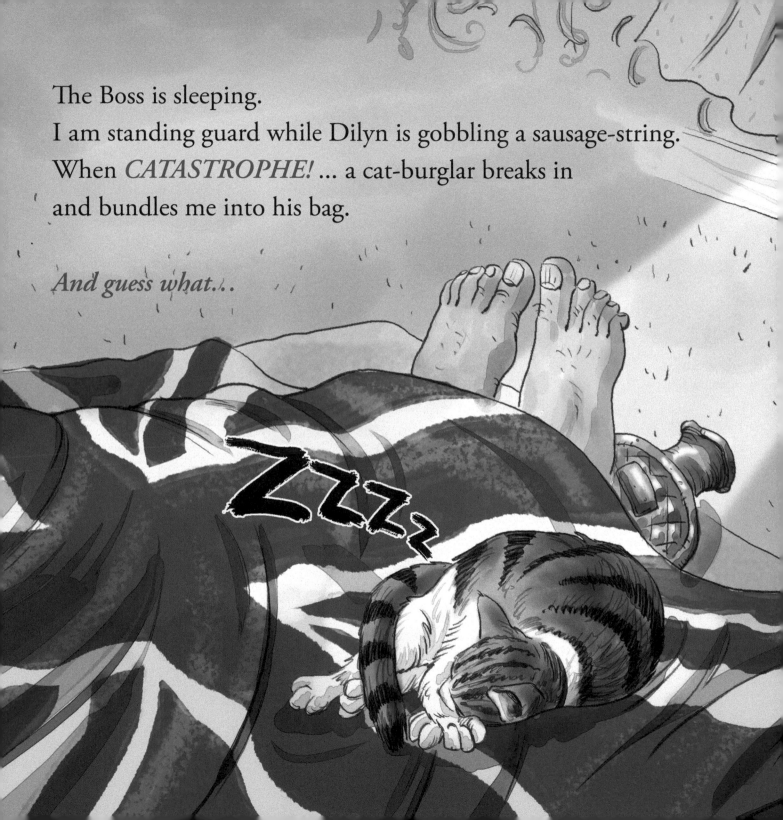

Dilyn starts chasing his tail
around the cat-burglar and ties him up
in the sausage-string.

WHIZZ!
WHIZZ!
WHIZZ!

The cat-burglar falls
on his bum…

BUMP!

Dilyn starts chewing and I jump out of the bag.

Woof Woof Meow Meow

All this cat-motion woke the Boss.

He calls the police who arrest the cat-burglar. The Boss says,

*"You are the best security guards
I have ever had."*

Catching Scoreboard

Dilyn   Palmerston   Gladstone

~~10~~   12   5

Squeaky
toys
don't count

 Matador